It's time for an ADVENTURE,

EGMONT

We bring stories to life

First published in Great Britain 2013 by Egmont UK Limited
The Yellow Building, 1 Nicholas Road, London W11 4AN

Baby Jake characters and logo © Darrall Macqueen Limited
2013. Baby Jake is a trademark of Darrall Macqueen
Limited. Licensed by BBC Worldwide Limited.
BBC logo TM & © BBC 1996. All rights reserved.

ISBN 978 1 4052 6553 9
53803/1
Printed in Italy

FSC
www.fsc.org

MIX
Paper from
responsible sources
FSC® C018306

Wibbly, wobbly tomatoes!

And Baby Jake is wobbling too!

It's going to be a **garden** adventure!

Yummy!

Baby Jake is picking vegetables with Nibbles the Rabbit.

Hello, Nibbles,

Pop! Pop!

Nibbles loves popping up big, crunchy carrots!

Pop! Pop!

WOW! These peas are even better for **popping!**

You're very good at **popping** pea pods Jakey.

The **popping** peas **pop** and **hop!**

Baby Jake wants to sing with you –
You know the words,
you used to sing them too ...

Yacki, yacki, yoggi – doo, doo, dee!

Bah, bah, bah, beep beep – noo see.

Yacki, yacki, yoggi – moo moo moo!

That's just what we love to do!

Yacki, yacki, yoggi,
let's do it again!

Yacki, yacki, yoggi – doo, doo, dee!
Yacki, yacki, yoggi, beep beep – noo see.
Bah, bah, bah, beep beep – noo see.
Yacki, yacki, yoggi – moo moo moo!
That's just what we love to do!

Yacki, yacki, yoggi – doo, doo, dee!
Bah, bah, bah, beep beep – noo see.
Yacki, yacki, yoggi – moo moo moo!
Hope you love to do it too!

What a lot of peas you've **popped** Jakey!

A m**ou**n**ta**in of peas and you two are right at the top!

Oh no! You're not going to,

are you **Baby Jake?**

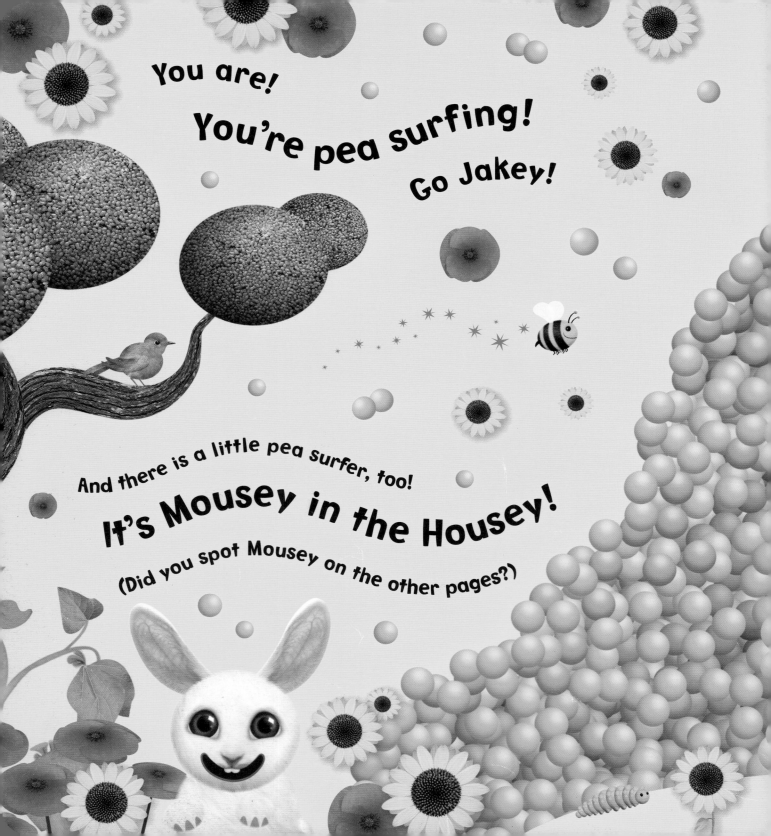

You are!

You're pea surfing!

Go Jakey!

And there is a little pea surfer, too!

It's Mousey in the Housey!

(Did you spot Mousey on the other pages?)

Wheeeeeeeee!

Toot! Toot!

It's Toot Toot and Jakey taking all the peas home for tea.

Bye bye **popping peas!**

Bye bye **Toot Toot!**

Bye bye **Nibbles!**

Bye bye **crunchy carrots!**

Bye bye **Mousey in the Housey!**

Goodbye!

Baby Jake and me,

Baby Jake and you,